ALL
ABOUT SPACE
SCIENCE

METEORS

Simon Rose

www.av2books.com

MEDIA ENHANCED BOOKS

AV² BY WEIGL™

ADDED VALUE • AUDIO VISUAL

Go to **www.av2books.com**, and enter this book's unique code.

BOOK CODE

H839335

AV² by Weigl brings you media enhanced books that support active learning.

AV² provides enriched content that supplements and complements this book. Weigl's AV² books strive to create inspired learning and engage young minds in a total learning experience.

Your AV² Media Enhanced books come alive with...

Audio
Listen to sections of the book read aloud.

Key Words
Study vocabulary, and complete a matching word activity.

Video
Watch informative video clips.

Quizzes
Test your knowledge.

Embedded Weblinks
Gain additional information for research.

Slide Show
View images and captions, and prepare a presentation.

Try This!
Complete activities and hands-on experiments.

... and much, much more!

Published by AV² by Weigl
350 5th Avenue, 59th Floor
New York, NY 10118
Website: www.av2books.com

Library of Congress Cataloging-in-Publication Data

Names: Rose, Simon, 1961- author.
Title: Meteors / Simon Rose.
Description: New York, NY : AV2 by Weigl, [2017] | Series: All about space science | Includes index.
Identifiers: LCCN 2016054640 (print) | LCCN 2017005659 (ebook) | ISBN 9781489658180 (hard cover : alk. paper) | ISBN 9781489658197 (soft cover : alk. paper) | ISBN 9781489658203 (Multi-user ebk.)
Subjects: LCSH: Meteors--Juvenile literature. | Meteorites--Juvenile literature.
Classification: LCC QB741.5 .R667 2017 (print) | LCC QB741.5 (ebook) | DDC 523.5/1--dc23
LC record available at https://lccn.loc.gov/2016054640

Printed in the United States of America in Brainerd, Minnesota
1 2 3 4 5 6 7 8 9 0 21 20 19 18 17

032017
020117

Editor: Katie Gillespie
Art Director: Terry Paulhus

Photo Credits
Every reasonable effort has been made to trace ownership and to obtain permission to reprint copyright material. The publishers would be pleased to have any errors or omissions brought to their attention so that they may be corrected in subsequent printings.

Weigl acknowledges Getty Images, iStock, Alamy, Shutterstock, and NASA as its primary image suppliers for this title.

ALL ABOUT SPACE SCIENCE

METEORS

CONTENTS

Rocks from Space

A meteor is a streak of light in the sky. It is caused by a piece of rock from space that enters Earth's **atmosphere**. The rock's speed may be thousands of miles (kilometers) per hour. Moving through the air at high speed, the rock becomes very hot. That is why it shows up in the sky as a streak, or trail, of light. Meteor streaks are sometimes referred to as **shooting stars** or **falling stars**. Meteors usually glow for about a second. Only rarely will a meteor trail last for a few minutes.

Most meteors occur about 31 to 50 miles (50 to 80 km) above Earth's surface.

Space rocks are called **meteoroids**. Most of them never come near Earth. Meteoroids may be as tiny as a grain of sand or as large as a huge boulder. A few may even be the size of a house or bigger. The majority of meteoroids that enter Earth's atmosphere are small. Most of these rocks get so hot as they travel through the air that they burn up completely before they reach the ground.

Some meteoroids are bits of planets or moons that have been blasted off during collisions.

Extremely bright meteors are sometimes referred to as **fireballs**. They are also known as **bolides**. Some scientists use the name *bolide* only for a fireball that explodes or produces a noise that may sound like thunder. A superbolide is an especially bright bolide.

FLUORESCENT FIREBALLS

Meteors generally look white, but a fast-moving fireball may appear blue or green. This is because of a reaction between the air and the object's motion. Sometimes, the color of slower-moving fireballs depends on what the rock is made of. Meteoroids made primarily of iron may appear to be yellow. A meteor with high calcium content may look like a purple streak of light.

Meteors through History

For thousands of years, most people thought that meteors were just something that happened in the atmosphere, like lightning. Some people imagined that the streaks of light came from the clouds, like rain, snow, or hail. This way of thinking about meteors is why they have the name they do. The word *meteor* comes from a Greek word meaning "high in the air." The same Greek word is the origin of *meteorology*, the name for the scientific study of weather.

Earthgrazers are meteors that streak close to Earth's horizon.

Around the late eighteenth century and early nineteenth century, a few scientists proposed that certain rocks found on Earth actually came from space. Initially, the idea was rejected by the scientific community. The theory slowly gained acceptance, however, as scientists began to pay more attention to meteors.

Small meteors only glow for about a second. Larger and faster meteors can be visible for up to several minutes.

American **astronomer** Denison Olmsted and French scientist Jean-Baptiste Biot were two researchers who made important discoveries. In April 1803, rocks rained from the sky at the French town of L'Aigle. Biot studied the rocks that reached the ground and found that they could not have originated on Earth. In November 1833, the Leonid shower, or Leonids, filled the sky with thousands of meteors. Olmsted studied the meteors' paths and concluded that they must have come from a cloud of particles in space.

Some scientists continued to believe that meteors originated in the atmosphere. However, as astronomers continued to study objects in space, more and more evidence built up that meteors came from beyond Earth's atmosphere. Eventually, Biot's and Olmstead's work formed the foundation of a new branch of science known as meteoritics.

Chinese astronomers were the first to record the **Perseids shower** in **36 AD**.

In 1839, Olmsted published a textbook named *An Introduction to Astronomy* for the use of his students at Yale University, where he was a professor.

Showers and Storms

On almost any night, a few meteors can be seen, as long as the sky is dark enough for good visibility. At certain times during the year, **meteor showers** occur. In a meteor shower, hundreds or even thousands of meteors can be seen in a single night. An especially intense shower is known as a meteor storm.

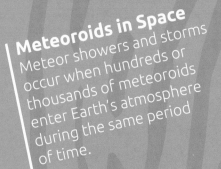

Meteoroids in Space
Meteor showers and storms occur when hundreds or thousands of meteoroids enter Earth's atmosphere during the same period of time.

Approaching Earth
When meteoroids enter Earth's atmosphere, they are traveling at a minimum of 25,000 miles (40,234 km) per hour. Friction with Earth's atmosphere causes the meteor to heat up and begin glowing.

Meteors
Soon, the heat caused by friction melts and vaporizes the surface of the meteoroid. The burning meteoroid leaves behind a trail of light, called a meteor.

Meteorites
The intense heat can cause meteors to break apart. Most pieces burn up. If the pieces land, they are called **meteorites**. Meteor showers can create hundreds of meteorites.

NAMING A SHOWER

The meteors in a shower usually originate, or "radiate," from one place in the night sky. This area is called the radiant. The shower gets its name from the **constellation**, or group of stars, in which the radiant lies. One of the most active showers that occurs regularly every year has its radiant in the constellation Perseus. At its peak, in August, the number of meteors in this shower can exceed 60 per hour.

Comets

Scientists now know that **comets** play a role in causing meteor showers. Comets are composed of gas, ice, and dust, along with rock. Some have **orbits** that take them near the Sun. When a comet comes close to the Sun, its temperature increases. Some of its icy material vaporizes, or turns into gas. As a result, the comet develops a tail, which may be millions of miles (km) long. Also, bits of rock get left behind in the comet's path. This debris gradually spreads out along the comet's orbit. If Earth passes through the comet's orbit, some of the debris may enter the atmosphere at high speed and burn up, producing a meteor shower.

The Leonid shower, for example, is caused by Comet Tempel-Tuttle. This comet takes about 33 years to complete its orbit around the Sun. In some places along its path, there is a huge amount of debris from the comet. In years when Earth passes through such a spot, the Leonids can create an intense meteor storm. Halley's Comet, which

sweeps by Earth approximately every 75 years, is responsible for two annual showers. One is the Orionids, a shower that peaks in late October. The other is the Eta Aquarids in early May.

Halley's Comet is named after Edmund Halley, the first astronomer to calculate the comet's orbit.

THE PHAETHON PUZZLE

Occasionally, **asteroids** may also play a role in causing meteor showers. Unlike comets, asteroids are made up mainly of rock. One of the most active annual meteor showers, the Geminids, seems to be caused by an asteroid called 3200 Phaethon. Scientists are not sure how a solid asteroid could have a trail of debris that can cause a meteor shower.

One explanation proposed for the Geminids is that 3200 Phaethon is really a dead comet. In other words, it long ago lost its gas and ice. Its rocky part continues to orbit the Sun, as does the stream of meteoroids the supposed comet once produced.

Another theory suggests that the Sun is causing Phaethon's trail of meteoroids. Phaethon passes close to the Sun during its orbit. Some scientists think heat from the Sun is breaking off parts of the asteroid as it passes.

The first Geminids shower occurred in 1862.

Falls and Finds

E very year, millions of meteoroids fall into Earth's atmosphere. Most are simply bits of dust. Only some of the pieces of material entering the atmosphere are large enough to produce a visible meteor. Just some of the rocks producing meteor trails actually make it to the ground. Large meteoroids are more likely than small ones to make it all the way through the atmosphere. Some large meteoroids, because of their makeup, explode before reaching the ground. There are also meteoroids that vaporize when they hit the ground, leaving little trace of themselves.

Each year, an estimated 30,000 to 80,000 meteorites larger than 0.7 ounce (20 grams) in size survive the fall to Earth. Most of them are unlikely to be seen or found, since they fall in the ocean or in areas where no one lives. Meteorites that are recovered are called "falls" or "finds." Falls are meteorites that are recovered right after they are seen falling through the atmosphere or hitting the ground. Many meteorites are not discovered by people until long after they have landed. These are referred to as finds.

In 1947, a bolide exploded over the Sikhote-Alin Mountains in Russia. Many of the collected falls are now displayed in museums.

Most meteorites are thought to be fragments of asteroids or comets. A few discovered in Antarctica, Libya, and elsewhere are different. Their makeup suggests that they came from Mars or the Moon. Scientists think these rocks may have been blasted into space when a large object, such as an asteroid, hit Mars or the Moon.

In 2015, scientists collected 570 meteorite samples as part of the Antarctic Search for Meteorites Program. The samples were flown to the Johnson Space Center in Houston, Texas, to be studied.

The Makeup of Meteorites

Meteoroids from comets are often not solid enough to survive passing through the atmosphere. For this reason, most meteorites found on Earth are thought to be asteroid fragments. They are divided into three main types. These are called stony, iron, and stony-iron.

Stony meteorites contain minerals rich in silicon and oxygen, with smaller amounts of iron, magnesium, and other **elements**. Most belong to the group of meteorites known as chondrites, which accounts for about 86 percent of all meteorites. Chondrites contain small round glassy particles called chondrules. Stony meteorites without chondrules are called achondrites. They account for about 8 percent of meteorites.

Most meteorites have a burned exterior, called a fusion crust.

About 5 percent of meteorites are iron meteorites. In addition to iron, they generally contain a fair amount of nickel. These rocks are thought to come from the metal core of an asteroid. Stony-iron meteorites account for only about 1 percent of meteorites. They contain silicon-based stone and iron-nickel metal in about equal amounts.

Meteorites sometimes produce small, oddly shaped glassy rocks called tektites. Typically black or olive green in color, tektites are usually no larger than 5 inches (12 centimeters) in size. They are produced when a large object from space hits the ground with a great deal of force. The impact melts some surface rock and may toss drops of the resulting liquid material into the air. The drops cool as they fly, turning into solid tektites. The tektites may land a considerable distance from the impact point.

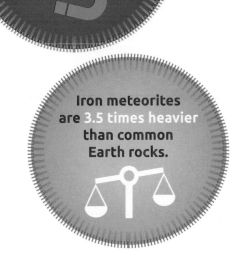

Unlike Earth rocks, most meteorites are magnetic.

Iron meteorites are 3.5 times heavier than common Earth rocks.

Moldavite tektites are green and translucent. They are often used in jewelry.

Impact Craters

When a large object from space hits the ground with great force, the impact usually forms a crater. A crater is a bowl-shaped or saucer-shaped hollow in the ground. Very large impact craters are sometimes called basins. Meteorite craters have been found on every continent except Antarctica. They may well exist in Antarctica, too, but the ice covering the continent makes it difficult to definitely prove their presence.

More than 190 impact craters have been identified on Earth. The Moon and some other bodies in the **solar system** each have many more. One reason why Earth has relatively few is that most meteoroids burn up before they can smash into the ground. Small objects that do make it to the surface may be slowed by the air to such an extent that they do not hit the ground hard enough to produce a crater. On the other hand, the air cannot significantly slow down a massive object that enters the atmosphere at a high speed. Such an object will very likely produce a crater if it hits the ground.

Over time, impact craters can fill with water and become lakes. Lonar Lake in Maharashtra, India, formed after a meteorite hit the surface there 35,000 to 50,000 years ago.

There is another major reason why relatively few craters are seen on Earth. Many craters formed by impacts in the past have disappeared. The rims of craters may be eroded, or worn away, by wind or moving water. In addition, Earth's layer of surface rock is affected by forces from below, which sometimes cause land to sink beneath the ocean.

The largest known impact crater on Earth is the Vredefort Dome, southwest of Johannesburg, South Africa. About 2 billion years ago, the area was hit by a huge object that made a crater roughly 185 miles (300 km) wide. The object that produced the Vredefort Dome may have been as much as 6 miles (10 km) wide. Rock below the surface was pushed down by the impact and then rebounded to produce a raised rock "dome." Most of this dome eroded away over millions of years. A ring of hills about 43 miles (70 km) wide is about all that can be seen of the Vredefort Dome today.

The remains of an ancient impact crater, such as the Vredefort Dome, are called an *astrobleme*, which is a Greek term meaning "star wound."

Major North American Craters

The best-preserved large impact crater on Earth is in northern Arizona, about 35 miles (56 km) east of Flagstaff. Known both as Meteor Crater and as Barringer Meteorite Crater, it is about 0.75 mile (1.2 km) wide and 600 feet (180 meters) deep. It was formed about 50,000 years ago by an iron meteorite that was about 160 feet (50 m) wide. The meteorite probably disintegrated when it hit the surface, with most of it spreading across the landscape in fine metallic particles.

Scientists believe the Barringer Meteorite Crater grew new vegetation and supported animal life within 100 years after the meteorite hit.

THE CORE OF A CRATER

In 2016, scientists Joanna Morgan and Sean Gulick led an offshore drilling operation in the Chicxulub Crater. For seven weeks, they drilled 4,265 feet (1,300 m) into the center of the crater. Their drill brought up core samples of rock.

The core samples will take many years to study, but the rock has already provided clues as to what happened after the meteorite hit Earth. The samples confirm the meteorite caused a mass extinction. They also show that within 10,000 years, the impact crater became a habitat for disaster species to live. Disaster species are animals that thrive in stressed environments. Later, new life forms began to develop.

The Chicxulub Crater measures about 110 miles (180 km) across, but it cannot be seen. It was formed 65 million years ago and today lies beneath Mexico's Yucatán Peninsula and the Gulf of Mexico. The impact that caused it may have resulted in the disappearance of half of all the species, or types, of plants and animals then in existence. The species that died out included most types of dinosaurs.

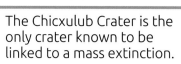

The Chicxulub Crater is the only crater known to be linked to a mass extinction.

Scientists believe that the object that created the Chicxulub Crater must have been huge. It may have been 6 to 9 miles (10 to 15 km) across. It smashed into Earth with an estimated force 2 million times greater than the largest nuclear bomb ever tested. This colossal impact likely caused wildfires, earthquakes, and volcanic eruptions. Huge clouds of ash probably covered the planet for several years, blocking sunlight and causing a drastic drop in temperature.

Craters on Other Worlds

Impact craters are found on many bodies in the solar system. They cover the planet Mercury, most asteroids, and the majority of moons circling planets. Earth's Moon is covered with craters. Unlike Earth, it has virtually no atmosphere to protect it from impacts, and there is no wind or rainfall to erode the craters. The Moon also has a super-sized impact crater, near its south pole. This basin is known as South Pole–Aitken. It is about 1,600 miles (2,600 km) wide.

Like Earth, the planets Mars and Venus have relatively few craters. Impact craters on these planets tend to become buried or eroded over time. The planets Jupiter, Saturn, Uranus, and Neptune do not have craters. They are mainly made of gas. They do not even have a surface like Earth's on which craters can be formed.

Mercury is covered in two kinds of craters. Primary craters were caused by meteorites. Secondary craters formed when Mercury's volcanoes spat out rocks that fell back down and hit the surface.

There are some enormous craters in the solar system that are known or believed to be the result of meteoroid impacts. Many scientists think, for instance, that an impact basin may cover most of the northern **hemisphere** of Mars. Sometimes called the Borealis Basin, it is about 5,300 miles (8,500 km) wide and 6,600 miles (10,600 km) long. The floor of the basin is 2.5 to 5 miles (4 to 8 km) lower than the planet's southern hemisphere.

Mars has some smaller, but still huge, features in its southern hemisphere that many scientists believe are impact craters. One is the Hellas Basin, which is more than 1,300 miles (2,100 km) wide. Another is the Argyre Basin, measuring roughly 1,100 miles (1,800 km) across.

Mars has at least 635,000 impact craters.

Working with Meteors

Several types of careers are available for people interested in studying meteors, meteorites, or meteoroids. These jobs require a strong background in science and, usually, one or more university degrees. In addition to getting an advanced degree, people often begin their careers with a couple of years of postgraduate training.

METEORITICIST QUALIFICATIONS

EDUCATION
Meteoriticists must first gain a bachelor's degree in geology. A master's or doctorate degree specializing in meteorites is then required to be a meteoriticist.

RESEARCH
Meteoriticists are expected to share their findings with others. This involves writing academic papers on their research methods and results.

TECHNOLOGY
Advanced equipment is used to weigh and classify meteorites. **Microprobe technology** is often used to identify the different metals within the meteorite. Meteoriticists must be capable of using this equipment.

DEDICATION
Meteoriticists often have to travel to find meteorites. The Antarctic Search for Meteorites (ANSMET) group collects meteorites from the Transantarctic Mountains.

WIDE RANGING INTERESTS
In addition to geology, meteoriticists need to be familiar with astronomy, astrophysics, chemistry, and the science of metals.

ASTRONOMER Astronomy is the study of the universe. Astronomers tend to specialize in a particular aspect of the field, such as planets, smaller bodies in the solar system such as meteors, the Sun, stars, the search for extraterrestrial life, or the origin of the universe. Many astronomers are professors at colleges or universities and do research as well as teach. Others work at observatories or museums.

ASTROPHYSICIST Astrophysicists are astronomers who focus on questions involving the principles of physics. Physics is the scientific study of **matter**, energy, forces, and the motion of objects. Some astrophysicists concentrate on the physics of a certain part of the universe, such as bodies in the solar system. Most astrophysicists teach astronomy, physics, or mathematics at a college or university while also doing research.

ASTROPHOTOGRAPHER Astronomy relies heavily on astrophotography, or the photography of celestial bodies. Astrophotographers need a knowledge of both astronomy and photography. Astrophotographers use a lot of specialized equipment such as powerful cameras and high powered lenses. The images taken by astrophotographers are studied by a variety of scientists and need to be of a high quality. The image data that they collect will likely undergo processing by sophisticated computers. Astrophotographers need to be familiar with the software and hardware involved.

Looking for Shooting Stars

On almost any night, it is possible to see a shooting star, as long as the sky is dark enough. The night sky in many areas gets a great deal of light from streets, vehicles, and buildings. In these places, it may be almost impossible to see any meteors. Moonlight can also interfere with the ability to see meteors. If the sky is dark but no meteor shower is occurring, it may be necessary to wait a while for a shooting star to appear.

Organizations such as the American Meteor Society (AMS) record meteor sightings from around the world. In 2015, the AMS received more than 4,000 reports of fireballs. Unlike normal meteors, a fireball is so bright that it can be seen during the day.

In 2013, a superbolide 30 times brighter than the Sun passed over Chelyabinsk, Russia. More than 10 meteorites were recovered from this event.

Meteor watchers do not need to use binoculars or a telescope. A meteor is usually easy to see with normal eyesight. Also, binoculars or a telescope make it hard to view large areas of the sky at one time. Looking at a broad area of the sky is the best way to see as many meteors as possible.

When there is a meteor shower, sky watchers should face toward its radiant in order to see the shower. For the Leonid shower, for example, the radiant is in the constellation Leo. People hoping to see Leonid meteors should look for that constellation.

AQUARIUS The radiant for the Eta and Delta Aquarid showers is the constellation Aquarius. The Eta Aquarids shower peaks about May 6–7, and the Delta Aquarids shower peaks about July 28–29.

PERSEUS The constellation Perseus is the radiant for the Perseid meteor shower. The Perseids is the largest annual meteor shower and peaks about August 11–12.

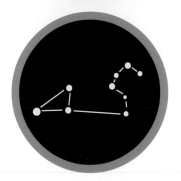

LEO The constellation Leo can be found between the constellations Cancer and Virgo. Leonid meteors are comparatively bright and peak about November 17–18.

Meteorites Timeline

Meteorite discoveries are fairly rare. Scientists can learn more about the solar system and Earth's history through the study of meteorites. This timeline shows important meteorite discoveries that have been recorded and analyzed.

1902 Ellis Hughes discovered a large iron meteorite in the Willamette Valley of Oregon. It weighs about 15.5 tons (14 tonnes). Now known as the Willamette meteorite, it is the largest meteorite ever found in the United States. Some scientists suspect the meteorite landed elsewhere and was moved to the area by massive floods at the end of the last **Ice Age**.

1895 American explorer Robert Peary took three large iron meteorites from Cape York, Greenland. He sold them to the American Museum of Natural History in New York City. The largest piece, called Ahnighito, or "the Tent," weighs about 34 tons (31 tonnes).

1920 The largest meteorite ever discovered was found at Hoba West, a farm in the African country of Namibia. It is an iron meteorite and weighs about 60 tons (54 tonnes). The meteorite has never been moved since its discovery, because it is so enormous.

METEORITES ON MARS

In 2005, the National Aeronautics and Space Administration's (NASA's) rover *Opportunity* found a meteorite the size of a basketball on Mars. It was the first meteorite to be discovered on another planet. It is believed to be a bit of another planet that was blasted into space. *Opportunity* photographed the meteorite and scanned it using a spectrometer, an instrument that analyzes an object's composition. It found the meteorite is made of nickel and iron.

Many other meteorites have now been found on Mars. In 2016, NASA's rover *Curiosity* found another iron-nickel meteorite. Scientists named it Egg Rock because of its shape and size. *Curiosity* found Egg Rock as it traveled up a mountain.

Curiosity carries a laser that can burn away thin layers of rocks. Using this laser, *Curiosity* was able to confirm the rock is a meteorite. It could also analyze its composition in detail.

1963 A large meteorite weighing about 22 tons (20 tonnes) was found in Greenland. Known as Agpalilik, or "the Man," it can be seen at the Geological Museum of the University of Copenhagen in Denmark.

1984 A meteorite named ALH84001 was discovered in the Allan Hills ice field in Antarctica. It is a volcanic rock thought to have formed 4.5 billion years ago on Mars. Scientists believe an asteroid hit Mars and blasted the rock into space. ALH84001 fell on Antarctica about 13,000 years ago.

2016 A meteorite was discovered near the town of Gancedo, Argentina. Experts weighed the meteorite at 34 tons (30.8 tonnes). Scientists believe it is about 4,000 years old.

Very rarely, meteorites cause damage to property. In 1992, a meteorite hit a car parked in a driveway in Peekskill, New York.

Meteorites found on Mars provide scientists with information about the origins of the universe. Some meteorites are millions or billions of years old. They give scientists a picture of the conditions soon after the universe formed. NASA hopes to one day bring a sample of a meteorite found on Mars back to Earth for further study.

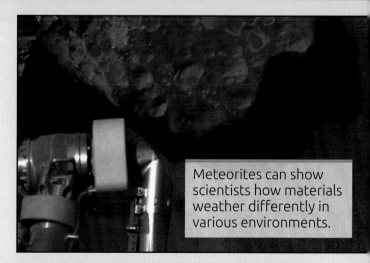

Meteorites can show scientists how materials weather differently in various environments.

Meteors Quiz

1
What is a meteor that streaks close to Earth's horizon called?

2
How many annual meteor showers does Halley's Comet cause?

3
What is the branch of science that studies meteorites called?

4
About what percentage of meteorites are chondrites?

5
Where was the largest meteorite on Earth discovered?

6
How many impact craters does Mars have?

7
When did the first Geminids shower occur?

8
What color are Moldavite tektites?

9
How fast are meteoroids traveling when they enter Earth's atmosphere?

10
What is the burned exterior of a meteorite called?

Answers
1. An Earthgrazer **2.** Two **3.** Meteoritics **4.** 86 percent
5. Hoba West, a farm in the African country of Namibia **6.** At least 635,000
7. 1862 **8.** Green **9.** A minimum of 25,000 miles (40,234 km) per hour
10. A fusion crust

Key Words

asteroids: rocky objects that have an orbit around the Sun and are bigger than a meteoroid but smaller than a planet

astronomer: a scientist who studies planets, stars, galaxies, and other objects in space

atmosphere: the layer of air that covers Earth's surface

bolides: fireballs, especially ones that explode or make a sound similar to thunder

comets: objects in the solar system that are composed of gas, ice, dust, and rocky debris

constellation: a group of stars that appear to form a shape or pattern in the sky

elements: the basic substances that make up matter

falling stars: meteors

fireballs: extremely bright meteors

hemisphere: half of a planet or other large object in space, such as the northern hemisphere or southern hemisphere of Mars

ice age: a period of time in Earth's history when ice sheets covered much of the planet

matter: a general name for the substance or substances that make up any object

meteorites: rocks that are found on the surface of a planet, asteroid, or moon and have fallen from space

meteoroids: rocks in space; meteoroids may be as tiny as a grain of sand or nearly as big as a small asteroid

meteor showers: the appearance of an unusually large number of meteors in the sky; some showers occur at the same time every year

microprobe technology: devices that study materials by measuring the radiation, or waves of energy, they emit

orbits: paths that bodies in space follow as they circle around other bodies, such as Earth's orbit around the Sun and the Moon's orbit around Earth

shooting stars: meteors

solar system: the Sun and all the objects that orbit it

Index

Log on to www.av2books.com

AV² by Weigl brings you media enhanced books that support active learning. Go to www.av2books.com, and enter the special code found on page 2 of this book. You will gain access to enriched and enhanced content that supplements and complements this book. Content includes video, audio, weblinks, quizzes, a slide show, and activities.

AV² Online Navigation

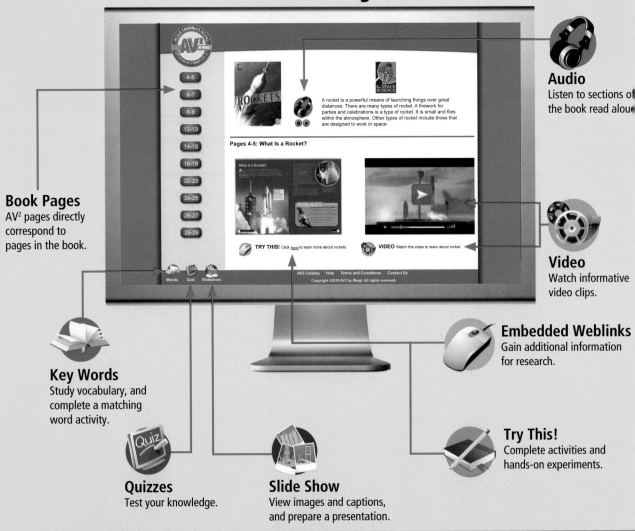

Book Pages
AV² pages directly correspond to pages in the book.

Key Words
Study vocabulary, and complete a matching word activity.

Quizzes
Test your knowledge.

Slide Show
View images and captions, and prepare a presentation.

Audio
Listen to sections of the book read aloud.

Video
Watch informative video clips.

Embedded Weblinks
Gain additional information for research.

Try This!
Complete activities and hands-on experiments.

AV² was built to bridge the gap between print and digital. We encourage you to tell us what you like and what you want to see in the future.

Sign up to be an AV² Ambassador at www.av2books.com/ambassador.